POCOYO™

Annual 2007

POCOYO ANNUAL 2007

A RED FOX BOOK 978 1 862 30199 3 (from January 2007) 1 862 30199 9

First published in Great Britain by Red Fox, an imprint of Random House Children's Books.

Red Fox edition published 2006

1 2 3 4 5 6 7 8 9 10

Text © Red Fox, 2006   Images © Granada/Zinkia, 2005

POCOYO™ © Zinkia S.L. Licensed by G.V.

The Pocoyo and series character logotypes are trademarks of Zinkia Entertainment S.L. and are used under licence.

All rights reserved. Red Fox books are published by Random House Children's Books, a division of The Random House Group Ltd, London, Sydney, Auckland, Johannesburg and agencies throughout the world.

THE RANDOM HOUSE GROUP Limited Reg No. 954009

A CIP catalogue record for this book is available from the British Library.

Designed by Dynamo Limited. Printed in Italy.

Contents

Say Hello to Pocoyo and His Friends

Hello, Pocoyo!
**Pocoyo is a friendly, curious little boy. He loves playing
with his friends and having fun. When you play with
Pocoyo, every day is an adventure!**

Hello, Pato!
Pocoyo's good friend Pato is a little bit shy. He likes planning, but things never turn out quite the way he wants them to!

Hello, Elly!
Elly is very graceful and gentle. She loves her friends very much, but sometimes she can be a bit of a know-it-all!

Hello, Loula!

Loula is Pocoyo's pet puppy. She is always ready to play, even when other people aren't. Loula adores Pocoyo and knows just how to make him laugh!

Hello, Cloud!

Little Cloud is Pocoyo's newest friend. He is full of fun and mischief!

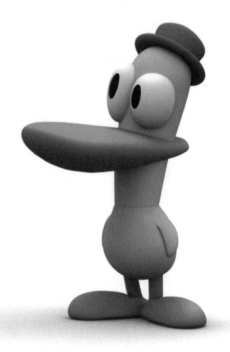

Hello, Sleepy Bird!

Sleepy Bird is very, very sleepy. Sometimes it seems as if she only wakes up to turn off her alarm clock!

The Big Sneeze

1 Hello, everyone! Today, Pocoyo, Pato and Elly are building a tower.

2 Whoops, careful!
It looks like it might topple over . . .
Phew! Well done, Pocoyo!

3 Pocoyo, Pato and Elly are all taking turns to put a block on top. Pocoyo has a turn, then Pato has a turn . . .

4 Now it's Elly's turn!
Elly is adding an orange block. But . . .

5 . . . ATCHOO!
Oh dear. That was quite a sneeze.

6 Never mind, all the friends can help build the tower again. Everyone has a go! What a lovely tall tower, Pocoyo!

7 Pato puts a blue block right on top. But can you guess what's going to happen?

8 ATCHOO!
Yes, Elly has sneezed again!

9 Whoops! I wonder where Pato has gone.
Can you see him?

10 Yes, you've found him!
Well done.

11 Oh, Pato, don't be cross.
People – and elephants – can't help it when they sneeze.

12 I think Elly might have a cold.
Where could she go to feel better?

13 That's right. Elly should go to bed. Resting is a very good thing to do if you have a cold.

14 Now Pocoyo and Pato can build the tower without any sneezes knocking it over.

15 But oh dear, I think Pato may have caught Elly's cold. Watch out!
Aaah . . . aaah . . . CHOO!

16 Maybe Pocoyo and his friends should build a tower another day!

Pocoyo Loves Colours!

Pocoyo is finding out about colours with his blocks.
Are you going to help him?
Tell Pocoyo what all the colours are.

Pocoyo and his friends are building a
very tall tower!
Now Pocoyo is adding a **YELLOW** block.

It is Pato's turn next. What colour
is his block?
Yes, it's **BLUE!**

Now it's Elly's turn.
Elly adds an **ORANGE** block.
Oh, isn't that fun!

Here comes Loula chasing her **RED** ball.
Oops! All the blocks have fallen down!

Odd One Out

Pocoyo has been taking photos of his friends!
Look at these pictures of Sleepy Bird.
Point to the photo that is the odd one out and say why.

Pocoyo's Favourite Words

B is for Blocks.
Here are some more things Pocoyo likes to play with.
Colour in the ones that begin with the letter B.

Ball

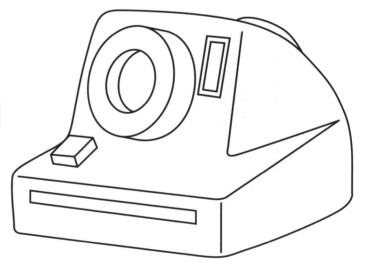

Camera

16

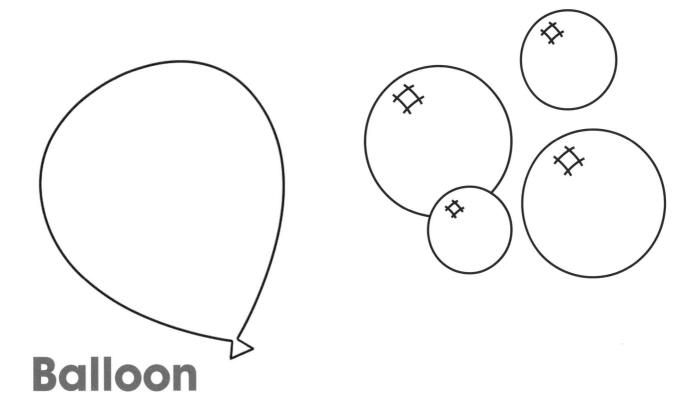

Bubbles

Balloon

Radio

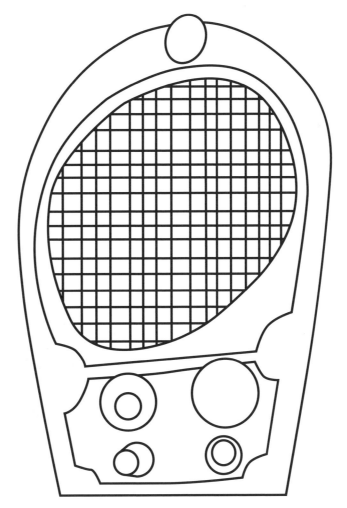

Swept Away

1 Hello, Pocoyo!
Pocoyo is building things today!
There's nothing more fun than building a nice tall tower . . .

2 . . . Except for knocking it down!
Today Elly is coming to play!
Perhaps we should tidy up before she arrives.

3 Can you see anything that might help Pocoyo tidy up?
Yes! A broom!
Do you know how to use a broom, Pocoyo?

4 Well, that's not what brooms
are usually used for.
But it does look like fun!
Do you know what Pocoyo is
pretending the broom is?

5 That's right! Pocoyo is pretending the broom is a horse!
Cowboy Pocoyo on a horse!

6 Now Pocoyo is a hockey
player, and the broom is his
hockey stick!
Pocoyo shoots! He scores!

7   That was wonderful, Pocoyo.
Oh! Do you know what Pocoyo is pretending the broom is now?
Yes! It's a guitar! Pocoyo is making music!

8 But something is wrong. Brooms make things tidier.
But it's not very tidy here! Wasn't there something we
were supposed to be doing?

9 That's right! We were tidying up!
Elly is coming over to play and she'll be here any second!

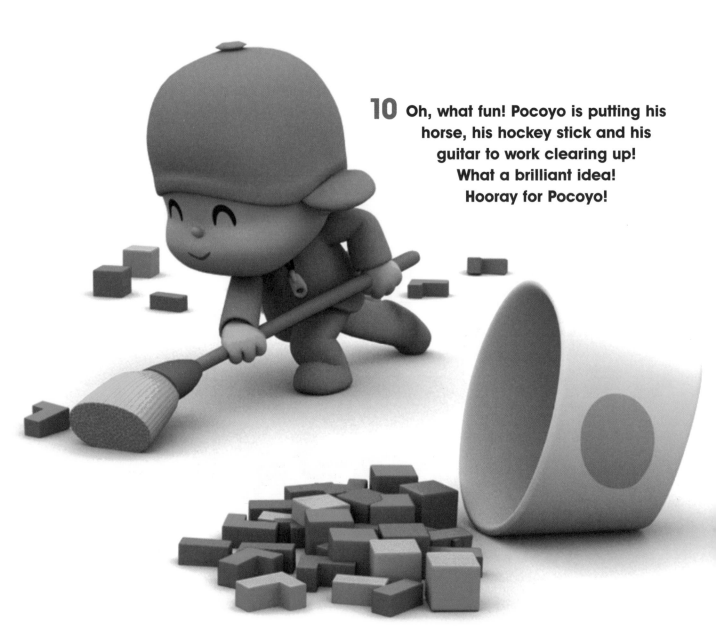

10 Oh, what fun! Pocoyo is putting his
horse, his hockey stick and his
guitar to work clearing up!
What a brilliant idea!
Hooray for Pocoyo!

11 Tidying up flies by when you're having fun!
And just in time for Elly's visit.

12 Tidying up can be fun, with a little imagination . . .
. . . And it looks like there's still more fun to be had!

Dot to Dot

Yee-hah! Oh, what fun!
Join the dots to find out what Pocoyo is playing with!

Which Way, Elly?

Elly is going to play with Pocoyo.
Help her get through the maze to find her friend.

Tidy-up Time!

Help Pocoyo to tidy up. Count how many of each object you can see.
Then write the number in the box.

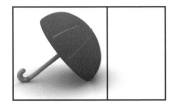 

Umbrella, Umbrella

1 Hello, Pocoyo!
What a beautiful sunny day.
But what's this?

2 Yes! It's an umbrella!
But what is an umbrella for? Pocoyo is
going to find out!

3 Uh-oh, it's getting a bit windy.
The umbrella is taking Pocoyo for a
ride! How exciting!

4 Whoops! How is Pocoyo going to get
down from there?

5 Well done, Pocoyo! Now, perhaps you should take another look. What else could an umbrella be used for?

6 Wait a minute, can you hear something? Quack, quack, quackity quack! It's Pato!

7 Quick, hide! But where?

8 Under the umbrella! What a good idea. Very good, Pocoyo!

9 Poor Pato. He can *hear* someone giggling. But he can't *see* anyone.

10 **SURPRISE!**

11 Oh dear. Poor Pato was so surprised he jumped and landed right inside the umbrella!

12 Here comes Elly! Maybe Elly knows what an umbrella is for.

13 Oh, Elly, what a wonderful way to use an umbrella! But wait. Can anyone hear thunder?

14 I think Pocoyo and his friends are about to get very wet. Can you think of anything that would keep them dry?

15 Yes! The umbrella! That's right, Pocoyo! Umbrellas keep you dry!

16 Hooray for Pocoyo! And for umbrellas!

Here Comes the Rain!

Pocoyo's umbrella is red. What colour umbrella would you like? Use your crayons to make your very own umbrella. The shape is already there to help you. Add some shapes and patterns too!

Hide-and-Seek

Oh, what fun! Pocoyo and his friends are playing hide-and-seek.
Look at the pictures and answer the questions.

Who is hiding behind the tree?

Where is Loula hiding?

Who is upside down in the flowers?

Can you spot Sleepy Bird?

Colouring Fun

Pocoyo and his friends are making music with the Ball Orchestra.
Use your crayons to finish the picture.

A Present for Elly

1 Hello, everyone!
Oh, look! It's someone's
birthday today.
Can you guess whose?
Yes! Today is Elly's
birthday. And she's having
a party later!

2 How exciting! Pocoyo is going to
make a present for Elly.
The party starts very soon, so
he'd better get going!

3 What's this? Oh, how wonderful!
It's a field of shapes!
There are lots of different colours and sizes!
I wonder why Pocoyo has come here.
Can you guess?

4 Yes! Pocoyo is going to make a present
for Elly out of all the lovely shapes!
What a nice idea. Oh! That's a good
start. A big pink ball!

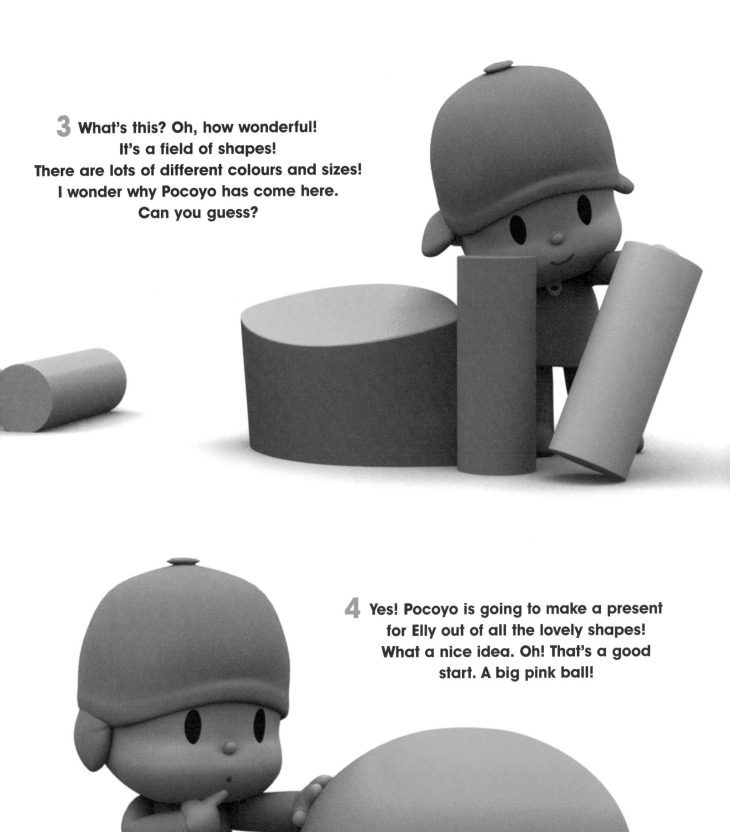

37

5 What shape are you going
to use next, Pocoyo?
This is so exciting!

6 What do you think Pocoyo
has made for Elly?
It's big, it's pink and it's a
present for Elly.
Can you guess what it is?

7 Yes, it's an elephant!
An Elly for Elly!
But something is missing . . .

8 Can you help Pocoyo work
it out? What's missing?
Yes, that's it. Well done!
Elly needs a trunk!
Do you know where it
goes, Pocoyo?

9 Oh, that does look funny, Pocoyo. But do you think that's the right place for Elly's trunk?

10 Where does Elly's trunk *really* go? Perfect!

40

11 Well, isn't that marvellous!
And just in time for her party.
Come on! It's time to go!

12 Elly loves her birthday present!
Let's all say happy birthday, too.
"Happy birthday, Elly!"
Hooray for Pocoyo! And hooray for parties!

Balloons Galore!

What beautiful balloons!
Who is holding the blue balloon? Follow the red wiggly
line with your finger to find out.
Now follow the other wiggly lines to find out which
colour balloon each friend has!

A Mystery Most Puzzling

1 Hello, Pocoyo!
Pocoyo has something to show you.
Do you know what it is?

2 It's a camera!
What is he taking pictures of?
A tree!

3 What else is Pocoyo going to take a photo of? Can you guess? Yes! He's going to take a photograph of the apple.

4 But oh no, where's the camera?
Someone has taken it. But who?
I think we need some clues!

5 Look, our first clue!
The person with the camera has left us a clue!

6 It's a photograph of a big pink foot.

7 Whose big pink foot could it be?
Is it Loula's?
No! It's not the same.

8 Look, another clue!
Another photograph!
It's something with wheels.

9 Whose wheels are those?
Are they the wheels on Pato's
skateboard?
No! They're not the same.

10 So, Loula hasn't got the camera and
Pato hasn't got it. Who can it be?
It's a mystery!

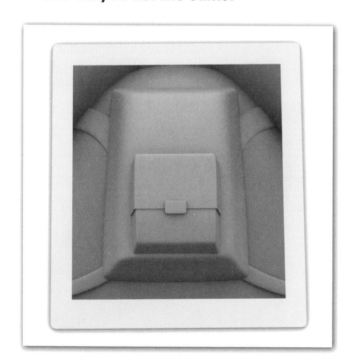

11 Look, Pocoyo, another clue!
It's a photograph of a blue backpack.
Whose blue backpack is it?

12 Who do we know who has a big pink
foot, rides something with pink
wheels and has a blue backpack?

13 Can you help Pocoyo?
Who do you think has the camera?

14 Yes, Elly!
Hooray for Pocoyo! He has found the camera!

15 Oh, what a good idea! Pocoyo is going to take a photo of his friends.
Smile, everyone!

16 What a lovely photo!

What's the Word?

Elly is learning some new words.
Look at the pictures and say the words.
Then copy over the dotted lines with your pencil.

Pocoyo is going to eat an

apple

Loula is playing with her

ball

Elly is wearing a stripy

hat

Sleepy Bird's home is in a

tree

Match the Pairs

Pocoyo has found some more clues.
Help him to match them into pairs.
Draw lines between the pairs and say what they are.

Pato's Picture Puzzle

These pictures look just the same,
but there are five differences between them.
Find all the differences and say what they are.

A Little Cloud

1 Hello, Pocoyo!
Pocoyo is going to have
a lot of fun today.
He's going to play with
his friend Pato.

2 But what's this? A shadow! And it seems to
be following Pocoyo.
Can you guess what's making the
shadow?

3 Yes, it's a little grey cloud!
Pocoyo doesn't like being
under the cloud.

4 Look! He's trying to get away from it.
But the little cloud is following
Pocoyo, and it's giggling!

5 Here's Pato! But oh dear, it looks like Pato doesn't want to play with Pocoyo. Nobody wants to be under the cloud.

6 The little cloud is chasing Pocoyo! Round and round! Round and round! Pocoyo can't get away!

7 What is Pocoyo doing now?
Oh, Pocoyo is shouting at the cloud.

8 Don't be cross, Pocoyo!

9 Oh no, the little cloud looks sad. Poor cloud. What will Pocoyo do now?
Ah, Pocoyo has an idea. Can you help him call the cloud?

"Cloud!"

10 Look! The little cloud has come down.
Perhaps it just wants a friend?
Ah, Pocoyo is giving the cloud
a lovely big hug.

11 Oh, what fun! Pocoyo's new friend is giving him a ride! The little cloud wants to give Pato a ride too.

12 Look, Elly! Look, Loula! Nothing brightens up your day like making a new friend!

Goodbye, Pocoyo!

It's time to say goodbye to Pocoyo and his friends!
Fill in the letters that are missing from their names.

Goodbye, Po‍c‍oyo!

Goodbye, P‍a‍to!

Goodbye, E‍l‍ly!

Goodbye, Loula!

Goodbye, Sleepy Bird!

Goodbye, Cloud!

POCOYO™
Competition

Win a fabulous set of Pocoyo plush, bath and interactive toys!
Win a brilliant Pocoyo DVD
Win a set of the latest Pocoyo books

All you have to do to win these fantastic prizes is answer this question:

What is the name of Pocoyo's pet puppy?

The first correct entry to be opened will win all the prizes and the next ten will win a DVD and a set of books. Send your answer on a postcard with your name and address to:

Pocoyo Annual 2007 Competition (HF)
Random House Children's Books, 61-63 Uxbridge Road, London W5 5SA

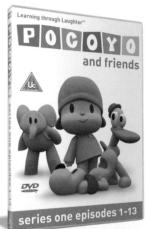

Learning is Fun with Pocoyo

Have more fun with Pocoyo in this brilliant range of board books and lift-the-flap storybooks!

P O C O Y O™
and Friends

A first book of friendship

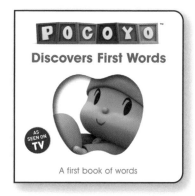

P O C O Y O™
Discovers First Words

AS SEEN ON TV

A first book of words

P O C O Y O™
Can Count

AS SEEN ON TV

A first book of numbers

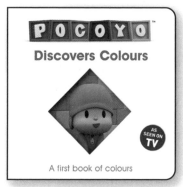

P O C O Y O™
Discovers Colours

AS SEEN ON TV

A first book of colours

P O C O Y O™
and the Camera

AS SEEN ON TV

Lift the FLAPS!

P O C O Y O™
and the Toppling Tower

AS SEEN ON TV

Lift the FLAPS!

Coming Soon

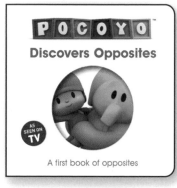

P O C O Y O™
Discovers Opposites

AS SEEN ON TV

A first book of opposites

P O C O Y O™
Discovers Shapes

AS SEEN ON TV

A first book of shapes

P O C O Y O™
Plays Hide-and-Seek

AS SEEN ON TV

Lift the FLAPS!

P O C O Y O™
Ready, Steady, Go!

AS SEEN ON TV

Lift the FLAPS!